STONE ARCH BOOKS
a capstone imprint

Cheerleading Really Is a Sport

by Julie Gassman

illustrated by Jorge Santillan

Sports Illustrated KIDS

STONE ARCH BOOKS
a capstone imprint

VICTORY SCHOOL SUPERSTARS

Sports Illustrated KIDS *Cheerleading Really Is a Sport*
is published by Stone Arch Books — A Capstone Imprint
1710 Roe Crest Drive
North Mankato, MN 56003
www.capstonepub.com

Art Director and Designer: Bob Lentz
Creative Director: Heather Kindseth
Production Specialist: Michelle Biedscheid

Timeline photo credits: Shutterstock/Charles Shapiro
(top); Sports Illustrated/Bob Rosato (middle left), John G.
Zimmerman (middle right), John W. McDonough (bottom).

Library of Congress Cataloging-in-Publication Data is
available on the Library of Congress website.
ISBN: 978-1-4342-2130-8 (library binding)
ISBN: 978-1-4342-2809-3 (paperback)
ISBN: 978-1-4342-4966-1 (e-book)

Summary: Alicia proves to her brother Danny that
cheerleading is a real sport.

Printed in the United States of America in North Mankato, Minnesota.
092018   000964

TABLE of CONTENTS

ALICIA GOHL

AGE: 10   **SPORT:** Cheerleading

SUPER SPORTS ABILITY: The sky is the limit for Alicia's super jumping.

ALICIA

CARMEN

DANNY

KENZIE

JOSH

ALICIA

TYLER

Brother Trouble

My twin brother, Danny, is in trouble
again. Since we changed schools, Danny
has been in trouble a lot. This is the third
time he skipped his chores. I know he is
tired from football practice, but he's not
going to get away with skipping his chores.

We started going to the Victory School for Super Athletes a month ago. All the kids at the school are amazing athletes. We all have a little something extra — a super skill.

Danny plays football. His super skill is speed. He can run the length of the field in seconds. Blink and you might miss him.

My super skill is jumping. I can jump
high enough to touch the roof in the gym.
Pair that with my loud voice, and you get a
pretty strong cheerleader.

"Daniel Gohl," starts Mom. Uh-oh. You know you are in trouble when Mom uses your full name. "This is the third time you've forgotten to take out the garbage. No video games for a week."

"That's not fair! I don't mean to forget," says Danny. "I'm just tired from practice."

He grabs the garbage and jets out the door. He's so fast that he's back before Mom has a chance to respond.

"You still have responsibilities at home," she says. "Dad and I expect you and Alicia to keep up with your schoolwork and chores. Being tired isn't an excuse."

Danny glances at me. "Of course Alicia gets her chores done. She doesn't have to work as hard at her practice," he says.

"What's that supposed to mean?" I say.

"Cheerleading isn't as hard as football. It isn't even a sport," Danny says.

Mom can see that I'm upset. "That's enough, Danny," she says. "Go start your homework. You are going to have a list of chores to tackle after dinner."

About My Squad

"It really bothers me when Danny puts down cheerleading," I tell Mom. "And he isn't the only one. The whole football team says stuff like that."

At one of our practices last week, a couple football players made fun of our dance. One guy even said we didn't belong at Victory, since we didn't play a real sport.

I tell Mom about my squad. Laney is a perfect dancer. She never makes a mistake.

Matt is super strong. He can hold anyone in a perfect lift forever. His arms don't even shake!

When Jenna is tossed, she spins so fast that she does at least five rotations.

"Everyone on my squad has a super sport talent. We all belong at that school. Cheerleading really is a sport!" I say.

"I know, I know," says Mom. "I have an idea."

"What?" I ask.

"You need to show your brother that being a cheerleader takes a lot of hard work," says Mom.

"How?" I ask.

"Well, you'll need to get permission from Coach Field, but that shouldn't be a problem." Then Mom leans in and tells me her plan.

The Challenge

The next day at school I wait for Danny by his locker. I've already talked to Coach Field. It's time to put my plan into action.

I stand there and practice what I want to say in my head. I can't wait! Where is he?

Finally, I spot Danny through the crowded hallway. He zips past everyone around him with his super speed. I feel a rush of wind as he reaches his locker.

"What's up?" he asks me.

"Hey, you don't have practice on Thursday, right?" I ask.

"Yeah, why?" Danny asks.

"Because you're coming to cheerleading practice," I tell him. Danny looks confused for a second, then he starts shaking his head.

"Why would I want to do that?" he asks.

"So you can see that cheerleading is hard work. I'm tired of you putting it down. But I know you won't stop until I prove how tough it is," I explain.

"I get what you're saying, but it's not going to work," Danny says as he puts his hand on my shoulder. "And I'm not going to do it."

I shrug off his hand. "You're just chicken," I challenge him. It sounds a little like a dare, and Danny never resists a dare.

"Chicken, huh? I guess we are supposed to workout on our own anyway. Running around with a bunch of cheerleaders might count, even if I don't sweat much. I'll be there," agrees Danny. "Now I have to get to history. See ya."

Yes! I think. That was the hard part. Now comes the fun part. And I grin all the way to science.

Practice with a Partner

Thursday's practice could hardly come soon enough. I'm so excited that I get to practice a little early. When I can, I love to spend time practicing jumps by myself.

Standing at one end of the basketball court, I jump and extend my feet in a perfect toe touch. I brush my head on the net. Oops! I need to watch where I'm jumping. I could have really hurt my head.

After a while, the rest of the squad starts arriving. But Danny is nowhere to be seen. Finally, I spot him.

Danny practically flies into the gym, he's going so fast. Still, he barely arrives in time for warm-ups. After a few laps and stretches, Coach Field calls us together.

"Listen up, team! Today we are going to focus on our competition routine," says Coach Field.

"First, I want you to practice the lifts. Alicia, Danny can fill in until your partner gets here. Can you tell him what to do?"

"Sure," I say.

I turn to Danny. "Okay, the first lift is easy. I'll just be standing on your arms. The hardest part is holding me steady."

"No problem," says Danny. I roll my eyes.

I explain how I will jump up and land on his shoulders. From there, spotters will help me into the next stunt.

"Normally when I jump up, I fly high enough to do a quick flip or twist — nothing too flashy — before landing on my partner's shoulders," I explain. "But that might be too much for you right away."

"I'm sure I could handle it," says Danny, "but whatever you want."

"Let's not risk it. Neither of us wants to get hurt before our big competitions this weekend," I say. "I'll count off to the jump. Remember, I'll land on your shoulders."

"I've got it, Alicia. Let's do this," says Danny.

"One . . . two . . . three!" I leap into the air and easily land on Danny's shoulders.

"Piece of cake," he says.

I ignore his smugness.

"Now take a look at Tyler over there."
I nod toward the pair next to us. "Two
spotters will help me up, but you need to
get ready to hold me like that."

Each spotter takes a foot, raises me up,
and passes my feet off to Danny. He wraps
his fingers around my toes.

I actually feel pretty safe up there. Maybe my plan won't work. So far, Danny has had no trouble keeping up.

But then I notice a little sway. Then a bigger sway.

"Danny, let my feet go. I'm getting down," I say.

I pop up in the air. With ease, I do a little flip before landing on my feet.

Danny turns to Tyler, who is still holding his partner up in the air.

"You must be the guy with super strength, huh?" Danny asks Tyler.

Tyler grins, "No, actually, I'm a perfect shot."

"What?" asks Danny, looking confused.

"Basketball is my main sport. I never miss a basket," explains Tyler. "During the off season, I join the cheer team. I love it! It's a completely different sort of challenge, you know."

Danny looks surprised, but he nods.

Team Gohl

Coach Field yells for us to move into position to practice our dance routine.

I nudge Danny, "Hey, we're going to work on our dance. I'm not sure how you can do it with us. Maybe this idea was silly. You can't really try cheerleading for just one day. You can go."

"If it's okay, I'll stay and watch,"
says Danny.

"You will?" I ask. Now I'm the one who is
surprised.

"I don't think I know as much about cheerleading as I thought I did," he says.

"Okay," I say. "Have a seat."

Danny watches from the stands as we go through our ten-minute routine. He watches our lifts and basket tosses. He watches our tricky stunts and our sky-high jumps. When we are done, he watches us do it all over again.

After practice ends, Danny walks up to me with a smile on his face. "Wow, that was great. I've only seen you cheering at games. I had no idea you guys did all that other stuff."

"That's what we do at our competitions. We have one on Saturday. You should come," I say.

"Maybe. Listen, you're the best jumper on the team. With jumps like that, you would be great in gymnastics. Why aren't you a gymnast?" asks Danny.

"Gymnastics might be a team sport, but you don't perform with your team. It's you out there by yourself. I like being part of a team. We all have to do our very best or no one does well," I say.

"Yeah, I like that about being on a team too," says Danny. "Ready to go home? You must be wiped out."

"I'm tired, but I'm going to stay a little longer," I say. "We're hanging posters on your teammates' lockers. We want to cheer you on for your big game on Friday."

"You put all those posters up? That's really nice," Danny says. "Thanks."

"No problem," I say with a grin. "You better get going. I'm sure you have some chores to do at home."

"Let me help! With my speed, we'll be done in no time," says Danny.

He zooms down one hallway, while I head down another.

I jump from locker to locker, and we're done in just a few minutes.

"Yes!" says Danny. "We broke the record, I'm sure!"

I laugh. "Three cheers for Team Gohl!"

Time to Compete

It's competition day, and our team is next. We're all lined up, ready to run onto the floor.

Tyler nudges me, "Look, your brother is here, and it looks like he brought some friends."

My eyes fly to the crowd. Sure enough, Danny is there, along with the rest of the football team.

I wave. I can't believe they actually came!

"Up next: Squad Superstar from the Victory School for Super Athletes," yells the announcer.

We run to the floor. For ten minutes, we hold the attention of everyone in that room. My favorite part is our big finish.

While the rest of the squad does lifts, I do a series of jumps. I do pikes, with my legs straight out in front of me. I do hurdlers, soaring over an imaginary track hurdle. I do double nines and form my arms and legs into number nines, one on top of the other.

I jump 25 times in all before I end with a triple back flip. I feel great as I land with my arms raised in a V above my head.

The crowd erupts, and everyone is on their feet. I'm pretty sure we'll take home the winner's trophy. But best of all, no one is cheering louder than Danny and his friends.

SUPERSTAR OF THE WEEK
Alicia Gohl

Cheerleaders have a hard time getting respect. But Alicia Gohl showed her brother and his friends that cheerleading takes training and hard work like any other sport. For that, she is our Superstar of the Week.

Alicia, why do you think that some people do not feel cheerleading is a sport?

Our most important job is to cheer on other athletes. So maybe some people forget that we compete too. Or maybe it is because we always look like we are having fun! Some people think that since we have big smiles on our faces, we must not be working hard. That's not true!

What do you do to get ready for a big competition?

We practice a lot in the days before. The night before, we all try to get lots of sleep. But usually I am so excited I have a hard time sleeping. Then for breakfast, I always have a grilled cheese sandwich. It sounds weird, but it is a good-luck tradition.

Does your super skill come in handy outside of cheerleading?

My mom always asks me to squash bugs on the ceiling, since it is so easy for me to reach them!

GLOSSARY

abilities (uh-BIL-i-teez)—skills or powers

competition (kom-puh-TISH-uhn)—a contest

double nines (DUH-buhl NINES)—cheerleading jumps where one leg and one arm are held straight out and the other leg and arm are bent in to form two "nines"

hurdlers (HUR-duh-lers)—in cheerleading, jumps where one leg is stretched out front and the other is bent at the knee, like you are jumping over a hurdle

responsibilities (ri-spon-suh-BIL-uh-tees)—duties

rotations (roh-TAY-shuhns)—complete turns around a center point

routine (roo-TEEN)—a performance that is carefully worked out so it can be repeated often

smugness (SMUHG-ness)—being so sure of yourself you annoy others

spotter (SPOT-er)—a person who helps cheerleaders during stunts to prevent them from getting hurt

toe touch (TOH TUHCH)—a cheerleading jump where the legs are straight out and to the side, with arms reaching toward toes

CHEERLEADING IN HISTORY

1898 The first cheerleaders lead crowds at the University of Minnesota. They are all men.

1905 Cheerleaders start using **megaphones**.

1919 A cheerleader at the University of Kansas plans a pep rally. He raises money to build a stadium.

1923 Young women are asked to be cheerleaders for the first time.

1935 Cheerleaders begin using pom-poms.

1939 **Women cheerleaders** are more popular now. Many men are away fighting in World War II (1939–1945).

1950 The National Cheerleading Association is formed.

1972 The **Dallas Cowboy Cheerleaders** appear for the first time. The squad is known for their dancing, beauty, and uniforms.

1982 Cheerleading spreads to Great Britain, Germany, Sweden, and Japan.

2008 As host of the Summer Olympics, **China** trains 200,000 cheerleaders. The squads cheer on teams from all nations.

JULIE GASSMAN

The youngest of nine children, Julie Gassman always wanted to be a cheerleader like her four older sisters. She finally got her chance when she cheered for the Tiger football, wrestling, and girls basketball teams in Howard, South Dakota. Today, she lives in southern Minnesota with her children, Noah, Sky, and Isla, and her husband, Nathan — a former cheerleader himself. Julie is also the author of *Nobody Wants to Play with a Ball Hog* from the Victory School Superstars series.

JORGE SANTILLAN

Jorge Santillan got his start illustrating in the children's sections of local newspapers. He opened his own illustration studio in 2005. His creative team specializes in books, comics, and children magazines. Jorge lives in Mendoza, Argentina, with his wife, Bety, and their four dogs, Fito, Caro, Angie, and Sammy.

VICTORY SCHOOL SUPERSTARS

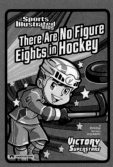

Read them ALL!

STONE ARCH BOOKS
a capstone imprint